THE
MEANEST SQUIRREL
I EVER MET

THE
MEANEST SQUIRREL
I EVER MET

by Gene Zion

Pictures by Margaret Bloy Graham

CHARLES SCRIBNER'S SONS, NEW YORK

ibble was a little squirrel
who lived in the woods with his father and mother.
On Thanksgiving morning, his mother
brought a basket up from the storeroom.

In the basket were pecan nuts,

walnuts and hazelnuts.

"Can I play with them?" Nibble asked his mother.

"Well," she answered, "if you're careful, you may.

But remember, these are not just ordinary acorns.

This is our Thanksgiving Dinner."

"I'll be careful," promised Nibble.

He took the basket of nuts outdoors
and played little games.
First he played Nuts in Rows.
Then he played Nuts in Circles.
He was playing Nuts in Little Piles
when he looked up and saw a stranger
coming up the path.

"Hello, young fellow!" said the stranger.

"My name is Mr. M. O. Squirrel."

"Hello," said Nibble. "I'm playing games."

"Playing games are you?" said Mr. M. O. Squirrel.

"Well now, isn't that nice! By the way,

did you ever play a game called Nut in the Hat?"

"No," said Nibble. "Will you show me how?"

"I'd be glad to," answered Mr. M. O. Squirrel.

He took off his hat and put it on the ground.

"Now you go first," he said.

"See how many nuts you can throw into the hat."

Nibble tried,
but he couldn't throw
any nuts into the hat.
It was too far away.

"Well, that's too bad," said Mr. M. O. Squirrel,

as he gathered up the nuts. "But now it's my turn."

One after another, he threw ten nuts into the hat.

Then without removing the nuts inside,

he put his hat back on his head, and said,

"Did you ever play a game called Basketnut?"

"No," said Nibble. "Will you show me how?"

"I'd be happy to," answered Mr. M. O. Squirrel.

He emptied the nut basket and put it up in a tree.

"It's very simple," he said.

"See how many nuts you can

throw into the basket."

Nibble tried,

but he couldn't throw

any nuts into the basket.

It was too high.

"Don't get discouraged," said Mr. M. O. Squirrel,
as he picked up the nuts Nibble had thrown.
"Practice makes perfect." Then he aimed and quickly
threw ten nuts straight into the basket.

Turning to Nibble, he asked,

"Oh by the way, did you ever play a game

called Basenut?"

"No," said Nibble. "Will you show me how?"

"Of course," answered Mr. M. O. Squirrel.

He picked up a stick and handed it to Nibble.

"Batter up!" he shouted.

"See how many nuts you can hit."

Nibble tried,

but he couldn't hit

a single one.

M. O. Squirrel threw them

too fast.

"Well you can't win 'em all," said Mr. M. O. Squirrel,

as he took the stick from Nibble.

Then he hit each nut a big wallop and one after another

they disappeared over a fence.

When they were all gone, he said,

"Well, goodbye now, I've got to run along."

Then he ran up the tree,

took the nuts from the basket

and put them into his pocket.

Then he jumped over the fence,

picked up the nuts he'd hit with the stick

and disappeared into the woods.

It all happened so fast,

Nibble couldn't believe

that he was alone once again.

He went into the house and told his mother

what had happened to their Thanksgiving Dinner.

"Don't worry," she said. "We'll think of something."

Just then, Nibble's father came into the kitchen.

"My, but I'm hungry today," he said.

"I could eat a ton of nuts!

Mother, when will dinner be ready?"

"I'm so tired of cooking, dear," said Nibble's mother.

"Let's eat dinner out today."

"Well," said his father, "that's an idea.

As a matter of fact, a chipmunk I met

told me about a little restaurant not too far away.

Let's give it a try.

We can eat our Thanksgiving Dinner at Christmas."

So they got dressed, locked up the house,
and off they went through the woods.
Nibble's father carried a bag filled with acorns
to pay for their Thanksgiving Dinner.

Soon they came to a big oak tree. One branch up
was a restaurant. It was called The Squirrel Cafe.
"This is the place," said Nibble's father,
looking at a card the chipmunk had given him.

They climbed to the restaurant,

went in, and sat down at a little table.

"Good afternoon," said the waiter,

as he bowed and handed them a menu.

"What a charming place!" said Nibble's mother.

Nibble's father read the menu aloud:

Thanksgiving
Dinner
Price.............20 Acorns

Imported PECAN NUTS
· · ·
Fancy ENGLISH WALNUTS
· · ·
Extra Large HAZEL NUTS

"That sounds just like the dinner we were
going to have at home," said Nibble's mother.
Nibble gulped and looked down at the tablecloth.
"I'm hungry," said his father. "Let's order."
They had dinner, but Nibble wasn't very hungry,
so his father ate most of his too.
"That was delicious!" he said
when he had finished.

Then they all got up to leave.

As they passed the kitchen, Nibble looked inside.

Suddenly his mother felt him tugging at her skirt.

"Gracious," she said, bending down,

"what is it?"

Nibble whispered something

in her ear.

"Oh my! You don't say!"

she said. "Oh my!"

In the meantime, Nibble's father

stood at the cashier's desk choosing a cigar.

Nibble's mother ran to him and whispered excitedly,

"Don't pay the check!"

"What do you mean, 'Don't pay the check!'?

What's wrong with you anyway?" he said.

"Don't ask me now," she said under her breath.

"I'll explain when we get home."

"I never heard such nonsense," said Nibble's father,

as he counted out sixty acorns and paid the check.

As they left The Squirrel Cafe

and started for home, Nibble's father said,

"Now tell me what that fuss was all about."

"I'll tell you some other time," said his mother.

"What *is* wrong with you two?" asked his father.

"Didn't you enjoy that fine Thanksgiving Dinner?"

Nibble seemed ready to cry.

That night, he went to bed but he couldn't sleep.

Finally he jumped up and ran into the living room.

"Papa!" he shouted. "I've got to tell you what happened."

First he told about Mr. M. O. Squirrel and the nut games

and how M. O. Squirrel had run off with all the nuts.

Then he told what happened in The Squirrel Cafe.

"I looked in the kitchen," he said, "and guess what I saw?

It was M. O. Squirrel!" he shouted, jumping up and down.

"He was chopping nuts and he was wearing a cook's hat!"

"M. O. Squirrel, M. O. Squirrel,"

said Nibble's father, scratching his head.

"Where have I seen that name before?

Aha! Now I remember!" he exclaimed,

as he took something out of his pocket.

It was the little card the chipmunk had given him.

Nibble's father read it aloud:

```
┌─────────────────────────────────────┐
│  ┌───────────────────────────────┐  │
│  │                               │  │
│  │   THE SQUIRREL CAFE           │  │
│  │   * * * * * * * * * * * * * *  │  │
│  │      Mr. M. O. Squirrel        │  │
│  │       Owner and Cook           │  │
│  │                               │  │
│  └───────────────────────────────┘  │
└─────────────────────────────────────┘
```

"Owner and cook, indeed!" exclaimed Nibble's father.

"Owner and *crook* is more like it. He took our

Thanksgiving Dinner, and then he sold it back to us!"

"Now calm down, everybody," said Nibble's mother.

"Maybe we'll think of what to do about it tomorrow."

Nibble's father and mother

kissed him goodnight

and he went to bed.

But in a minute, he was back in the living room.

"I know what let's do!" he said. "Let's go back

to The Squirrel Cafe and eat another dinner.

Then we'll run out without paying the check."

"Please go to bed, Nibble," said his father.

Nibble went to bed, but in a minute he was out again.

"I know what!" he said. "Let's stand under M. O. Squirrel's

window and miaow like cats. When he throws acorns

to chase us away, we'll pick up sixty and run home."

"Nibble, go back to bed," said his father.

Nibble went back to bed, but soon he was out again.

"I know!" he said. "Let's just climb in through

M. O. Squirrel's window, and take back our sixty acorns

while he's asleep."

"Nibble, you go to bed, or else!" shouted his father.

This time, Nibble went to bed and stayed there.

In a little while,

he fell asleep and dreamed all night long.

First he dreamed that he went to the police and told them about M. O. Squirrel. They arrested M. O. Squirrel, checked his paw-prints and found out his real name. It was "Mean Old Squirrel." He was brought to trial, found guilty, and the judge sent him to prison for sixty years. No one felt sorry for Mr. Mean Old Squirrel.

Then Nibble dreamed that the judge turned to *him* and said,
"Aren't you the one who runs out without paying the check?
And who imitates cats in the middle of the night?
And aren't you the one who goes in through windows
to help yourself to acorns? Aren't you? Aren't you?"
shouted the judge, jumping down and shaking him.

"Stop shaking me. Please stop shaking me,"

said Nibble, rubbing his eyes.

"But you must get up," said his mother,

shaking him again. "It's time for breakfast."

Nibble got up and dressed quickly.

"I'll be right back,"

he said to his mother.

"I've got to do something."

Then he ran down the path

through the woods.

Nibble ran all the way to the big oak tree.

For a moment, he stood looking up.

"I didn't think it was that high up," he thought.

But then he started to climb to The Squirrel Cafe.

When he got there, Nibble knocked on the door.

His heart pounded as he waited.

Finally the door opened

and there stood Mr. M. O. Squirrel.

Nibble spoke in a quiet but very firm voice.

"Mr. M. O. Squirrel," he said,

"give me back the sixty acorns

my father paid you for Thanksgiving Dinner.

You're the meanest squirrel I ever met—

and you know why too."

For a moment, M. O. Squirrel just stood

and stared with his mouth open.

Then, finally he spoke.

"Young fellow," he said,

"you're the *bravest* squirrel I ever met."

In a little while,

Nibble's father and mother saw Nibble coming home.

Behind him walked M. O. Squirrel, carrying a bag.

When they reached the house, M. O. Squirrel

put the bag down. Then he turned and ran back

down the path into the woods.

"Papa! Mama! Come and look!" shouted Nibble,

as he opened the bag.

"See!" he said, and he dumped out the acorns.

"I told M. O. Squirrel to give them back and he did!"

"Well, now I've seen everything," said his father,

as he stared at the acorns. Then he began to chuckle.

"Tell me," he said, "how did you ever get that rascal

to carry them home for you?"

"Well," said Nibble,

"I told him they were too heavy for me,

so he'd better carry them."

Nibble's father and mother

looked at each other and smiled.

Then they all went into the house

and had breakfast.

Early Christmas morning,

Nibble looked out of the window and saw

Mr. M. O. Squirrel walking up the path to the house.

He ran downstairs and opened the door.

"Merry Christmas!" said M. O. Squirrel.

"Here are some presents for you."

"Thank you," said Nibble. "Merry Christmas to you!"

They went inside and Nibble opened the presents.

There was a big bag of nuts with a note, which said,

"Please accept this Christmas Dinner—

from M. O. Squirrel (former sinner)."

There were a pair of skates and a hockey stick.

"Did you ever play a game called Nut on the Ice?"

asked Mr. M. O. Squirrel.

"No," said Nibble. "Will you show me how?"

"Of course I will," answered Mr. M. O. Squirrel.

And he really did.